# A
# VAMPIRE'S
# STORY

# A
# VAMPIRE'S
# STORY

SHELDON D. DOTTERY

MILL CITY PRESS

Mill City Press
555 Winderley Pl, Suite 225
Maitland, FL 32751
407.339.4217
www.millcitypress.net

Paperback ISBN-13: 978-1-66289-865-5
Ebook ISBN-13: 978-1-66289-866-2

# Table of Contents

# **Dedicated To**

Bobbie Jean Hadley

Dante Bell

Johan Williams

# Chapter One

# <u>The Rebirth</u>

Rumor has it we have been roaming this world for centuries; I was unaware of this until 2016. The only thing I knew of this species was what I saw on TV or in books I may have read; I never thought this "fictional" monster would enter my life and snatch it away from me. Sure enough, they exist; I am one of them now. Locking your doors and windows will not prevent us from entering your homes; a stake through the heart might slow us down but will not kill us.

Sunlight is your best weapon or beheading; creatures of the night are what some call us. Others may say we are misunderstood beings. I say we are the next scariest thing on this planet, next to Donald Trump being elected for office. If I could relive that night that I hate so much that night that I hate the most, that night when I was turned, I would change so many things.

I had a life before this; it was not the best, but it was mine, and I shared that life with two amazing people. My girlfriend Vanessa was a pure and genuine soul. Her skin was like gold, she had luminous green eyes and natural blonde hair as if it was dipped in clouds from heaven, and I loved how she represented her African roots out loud. My best friend Derek, I never met any Mexicans with the name "Derek" or expected him to have a simple last name like Graham, but here he is, and then there's me, a want-to-be pretty boy with locs draping down to the middle of my back as if I could be kin to Bob Marley.

1

Derek and Vanessa gave me the nickname "pretty boy" because I always wanted to keep my hair neat; I just wanted to always look presentable. We were a band of misfits, some would say. Vanessa was my everything, she was my world, and I was going to propose soon… Before I go any further, let me start from the beginning. I will start from the day when everything changed.

It was a day for celebration, Derek just passed his state exam to become a Certified Nurse Assistant. Vanessa just passed her last college final next stop graduation, and I finally scored big at a photo shoot for models with this big-time agency. It finally felt good to get noticed and receive a paycheck for my photography skills; now, I can pay our rent before Vanessa, and I get evicted.

Derek and I thought it would be good for all of us to go out and celebrate, especially since we rarely have good days. We wore our best outfits, called a cab, and went downtown to club "Reign." The music was great, the energy was great, our drinks were amazing, the entire vibe was perfect. 2 a.m. came around, and like most clubs, that meant it was time to go home. All three phones were dead, so we had to find a pay phone to call a cab; we decided to take a shortcut down an alley.

Thunder started to roar as we continued to walk; we saw three people toward the end of the alley. The rain started to fall, and it fell hard. As we got closer, it appeared to be an older man and two other men; the other two looked like they could be our age. The two men started to attack the older gentleman, so I decided to help; Vanessa and Derek tried to stop me, but the two guys ran off soon as I got closer.

The older gentleman looked homeless; I helped him up and said, "I'm sorry this happened to you. Are you okay?" he didn't make a sound. I helped him to his feet slowly, and when we made eye contact, his eyes were bright red, and his teeth were sharp enough to cut through metal; he grabbed both of my arms and said, "Thank you for helping me, now I welcome you to the family Michael," and he bit me. As I yelled for help, I began to feel weak, he released me from his grip, and I fell to the ground; the fight for my life had begun.

Derek and Vanessa rushed me to the hospital. Doctors tried every-thing they could to keep me alive but were also confused about my wound; two punctures to the neck just did not seem like a normal injury. Vanessa and Derek were in the waiting room; Vanessa was pacing back and forth, and then Derek shouted, "That old guy bit him on the neck! As if he was hungry, how does that small bite get us here?!" Vanessa says, "I don't know! and I don't care; I just want Michael to come from back there already; I need him to be okay."

Derek sits beside Vanessa and begins to comfort her. Doctors are doing all they can, but their efforts are no match for the supernatural, and after a few more attempts, I died. I was pronounced dead. Doctors returned to the lobby to deliver the news to Vanessa and Derek. Doctor Lynn says, "I am so sorry. We tried everything, but Michael did not make it." [Vanessa and Derek began to scream and cry] I awakened when I heard their cries, but something was new and different.

All my senses were different. They were heightened somehow. I could hear better, see better, even see through walls, and felt stronger. "What is this? What's happened to me?" I whispered. I then heard the Doctors from the lobby say, "Let's go prep the body." I quickly jumped out of the bed, searching for an exit. Footsteps grew louder; my best bet was to jump out of the window, and when I did, I ended up behind the hospital and landed in a dumpster.

I knew I needed to get away from that area, then a small voice in my head started calling my name "Michael…" the voice said. I started to look around, trying to figure out who was calling my name; as I con-tinued to look, I heard the voice again. "Michael…" it was calling my name repeatedly, growing louder and louder. "Michael, follow these directions, keep straight through the alley, cut across Brown Street, and I'll meet you at the park where you and Derek used to skip class."

I did just that: I ran through the alley and cut through the traffic on Brown Street. A car nearly hit me, but I made it to the park. "I'm here! Show yourself… I am unsure what the hell is going on with me…" "HELLO!" I yelled, but still nothing "AHH!!" I shouted out of frustration, then smoke appeared, and from the shadows came a man; he was 6'4, with black shoulder-length hair and creole.

He was walking with a beautiful woman on his arm. He greets me and says, "Sorry for the theatrics; I was a theater major before all of this… anyway my name Aries." Aries extended his hand to me, but I refused. "Well, that's rude of you, Mikey, but I'll let that one slide, so tell me, do you know why you're here?" Aries says. "No," I replied, "You're here because I am going to teach you the way of our world. Mike, my boy, our species is unique [dramatic pause].

We are hunters; now, some do it for survival, some for pleasure; I do it for a bit of both." "Our species? We are hunters. What the hell are you talking about? Are you crazy!? We! Are not the same; I don't even know what you are, or what I am for that matter, or Who you are," I said. Aries replies, "Who am I?" I replied, "Okay, man, whatever, what are you?" his teeth grew longer and sharper; his eyes turned red, and then he turned to the beautiful woman he came to the park with and bit her on the neck.

When he released her lifeless body to the ground, he turned to me with blood dripping down his mouth and said, "I'm a vampire." I was looking at her body on the ground in pure disbelief; Aries snapped his fingers twice at me and said, "Mike, are you with me?" I replied, "You killed her [pause]. Why?" Aries said, "I did that to show you what you are and because I was also hungry." I was standing there with a blank look. [Aries continued] "Look, all kidding aside, this is your life now; like it or not, you are considered a monster and will need to feed."

I am still slowly trying to process all this, and I replied, "I won't do that; I'll never kill people." Aries says, "You're in denial, but that'll change after a few days… quick better find a place to lay your head; the sun is coming up soon." Aries disappeared, four nights have gone by, and I have yet to feed on anyone; I started to feel weak to the point where I could no longer stand, I knew I had to find Aries.

In my search, I stumbled across a farm. I had not grown to take human life yet, so farm animals would have to do it for now. After one pig and two cows, I regained some of my energy. As I exited the farm, I bumped right into Aries, and without hesitation, I said, "I am ready to learn." Aries investigates the farm; he sees all the dead animals I just drained and says, "Animals? We must start somewhere."

# Chapter Two

# <u>The Teacher & The Student</u>

A couple of weeks have passed since I was turned, and since then, Aries has been trying to show me the "way of the vampire," as he put it, but I am still struggling with taking human life. For the time being, I've drank only the blood of animals such as deer, cows, etc. night after night, Aries and I were on the search for "prey," and so far, every time Aries demonstrates to me how and where to bite a victim, I back out of it.

One night, while Aries and I were out searching for potential victims, I began to take an interest in him. I had a lot of questions. "How is it so natural for you?" I said, "It hasn't always been natural... in fact, it was tough for me to take anyone's life, but after four victims, you start to get used to it...I was feeding on animals at one point, just like you, so I understand why you feel the way you do, which is also why I have been so patient with you." Aries replied.

"How did you transition from feeding on animals to feeding on humans?" I asked. "Human blood contains our thirst; animal blood only distracts it. I figured that out after biting my first human; animal blood will keep you content for a couple of hours, maybe a little more, but then you will need more. If you feed on two to three humans in one night, you'll be good for a few days until you need to feed again."

As the conversation continued, a girl looking to be between eighteen maybe twenty one years old showed up to sit in the park. I said to Aries, "My first victim." As I got into my predator mode, my senses picked up that the girl was sick. I hesitated, "I can't," I said; Aries replied, "Why Not?" I replied, "She's sick… she's already dying." Aries says, "You can sense that? If so, then put her out of her misery." I refused, and then we both left the area. Aries says, "You were so close.

Look, drink my blood you haven't fed in a few days." Aries extended his arm and said, "Drink from my wrist." As I bit into his wrist, the taste of his blood triggered memories from his past. Aries is shown hiding a book called "The Vampire Journal." I continued to feed until I had my feel, and once I stopped feeding, I asked, "What's the vampire journal?" Aries looked at me in total shock, and the two of us shared a moment of awkward silence.

"The Journal Aries, what is it?" I said, Aries replies, "How do you… It's nothing." I said, "If it's nothing, why were you hiding it." Aries quickly cut me off and said, "It's nothing you need to worry about; that was from long ago. Head to the mansion and go to your chamber. The sun will rise soon." The next night, I wandered the streets looking for my first official victim.

I stumbled across Club Reign, hesitant to go inside because all I could think about was the night I was turned into this, which is not a pleasant memory. This beautiful Nubian queen walks past me, instantly casting a spell on me with her hazel-brown eyes. That was more than enough of a reason for me to go inside. Music was playing, people were dancing, and I was searching for this mysterious girl I shared a moment with. I looked to the bar, and there she was.

I slowly approached her and said, "Hello, my name is Michael." She replied, "Hi, I'm Lydia." Her eyes had some hold over me, and I wasn't sure why or how. "Who are you here with?" I said. "Just my brother and two friends" She replied. "How about a dance?" I said, and she replied, "How about we leave here together instead?" We both smiled and made our way toward the exit; we were taking a shortcut back to her place and walking down the same alley where Aries turned me. I stopped to look at where Aries almost left me for dead.

"What's wrong?" Lydia said to me. "Nothing, I just hate this alley, is all," I said. "Interesting," Lydia said. "What's interesting?" I said. Lydia said, "Interesting that you hate this alley. Well, sorry, you're about to hate it much more." Two men appeared from behind a dumpster. One had a gun, and the other had rope; you would think I could've sensed them with me being a vampire, but I guess I'm still connected to my human nature of distraction that I didn't notice them. The man with the gun pointed it at me and yelled, "PUT YOUR HANDS UP NOW AND EMPTY YOUR POCKETS." I looked at Lydia and began to laugh. She said, "Hey! We're robbing you, you idiot; now do as he said!"

I continued to laugh. I then turned to the two men and saw Aries moving with stealth, slowly approaching the two of them; I then turned my attention to Lydia and said, "You're gorgeous. It's just sad none of you get to leave this alley and tell this story." She said, "We have the weapons. What do you have? GIVE US YOUR FUCKING MONEY."

As I continued to look at Lydia, my eyes began to glow yellow, my teeth grew & my rage was increasing rapidly by the second. Aries rushed the two men, putting both hands through their chests and ripping out their hearts. I rushed Lydia and quickly bit her on her neck, and she began to scream. I covered her mouth with my hand and drained her until I felt her life leave her body.

I dropped her onto the ground and turned to Aries; he looked very pleased. "How did it feel? Did you love it?" Aries said, "I need more... I need more," I said. The two of us prowled the city for more victims; by our third victim, I still had questions for Aries, questions he was trying to avoid, but these were questions I needed answers to; maybe I'll have to time it just right and figure out when it's appropriate to ask him anything.

With each passing night, I was growing stronger and stronger. Aries seemed to be proud, but I was feeding for survival. Aries was killing for pleasure and sport. Three months have passed, and night after night, I've learned something new. I am now in complete control of my vampire abilities, and one night, I finally found the courage to ask Aries more about this vampire journal.

"I am most impressed, Michael. You've turned out to be quite the vampire." Aries said. "Well, I've had an opportunity to work with a great teacher; thank you for putting up with me." I said.

# Chapter Three

# <u>Michael Vs Aries</u>

Weeks turned into months, months turned into years, and with time, I finally mastered the art of being a vampire. Remember when I told Aries he and I were not the same? Well, I meant just that. Aries and I did not share the same vampire abilities. For example, Aries could disappear by using fog as a distraction. I could only move extremely fast, fast enough that you'll never see me approaching, the proper term for this is called warping.

Also, Aries only possessed a heightened sense of smell when someone is near or if something doesn't feel right. I could do the same, but I could also detect your heartbeat, and if I looked close enough, I could see if you're ill; just a few minor differences, same monster but with different gifts. These various gifts are part of why some of you still have breath in your body today. It's because I pity you.

Another characteristic difference between Aries and I is we kill differently; yes, we both kill, but I kill with rules: no children, no elderly, and no people that are ill and already suffering, but when it comes to Aries, no one is safe, and that truly bothers me at times. At night, the city is our playground, picking off who we want whenever we want. Everything was ours for the taking.

Yet here I am with a mountain of questions for Aries that I hope he would give me straight answers to, but perhaps my approach has been too aggressive, and maybe I should start with small questions before we get to the tough ones. "How long have you been doing this?" I said to Aries. "Doing what?" Aries replied, "You know this whole vampire thing?"

Aries chuckles at my question and responds, "Honestly, only a little while... I was turned back in 1976." I was in complete disbelief with his answer, "You mean to tell me you've been a vampire for only forty-seven years?!" I said, "Is that a problem for you? Should I have been a vampire longer than forty-seven years?" Aries replied. "Well, you know, in the movies and everything, Vampires have been around for thousands of years, maybe even more." Aries chuckles again and says, "That's your problem right there, believing what you saw in a movie... A movie, a book, even a television series are all fabricated stories about us, and none of it is correct."

I was standing there just amazed about how much Hollywood lies, but let's be honest, are any of us shocked by Hollywood anymore. "That's interesting, so let me get this right. All those stories about Dracula are all lies, then, huh?" I said. Aries replied, "Dracula is very real; some of the stories told about him aren't all correct, but some aren't all the way incorrect either, if that makes sense." I looked at how serious Aries was with that response, and all I could do was laugh hysterically, "Is something amusing, Michael?" I just continued to laugh, not knowing that I was offending him.

Aries quickly warped in front of me, full of rage, and said, "I will not be mocked by you; do you think this is a game? Dracula is real! Not only is he real, but he is our king and the true prince of darkness, and you will show him the Damn! Respect he rightfully deserves." It was like I was staring into the eyes of Joe Jackson. Aries was full of anger and disappointment. "I didn't know... So, where is he?" I said. Aries replied, "He is off the radar; after being around for so long, he decided to rest for a while." I replied, "Fair enough, let's switch gears... what was your life like before this?" Aries replied, "Why all the sudden interest, huh? What is with all the questions! The only question you should ask is how you got so lucky to be given eternal life."

Aries quickly vanished. I guess I went too far. I did not see Aries for the rest of that night. I wasn't sure when I would see Aries again, but maybe it was a good thing he took off for a while. We've been hunting together for so long it felt good to do it on my own without being micromanaged, but I knew the next time I saw Aries, I would ask him about the journal and why he was hiding it. My thirst was satisfied, and the night was still incredibly young, so I decided to take on the town alone and mingle with the city's night owls.

I stumbled upon this Jamaican poetry club, and of course, it was open mic night, but luckily for everyone inside, I had no need for blood, so that meant all of us could enjoy this evening. There were many poets, poems, and artists; it was an amazing room to be in. As everyone made their way to the exit, a woman bumped into me and dropped her purse.

I picked it up for her, and as soon as I looked into her amber eyes, I knew I was trapped; her smile was bright enough to light up a room. I quickly introduced myself. "Hi, I'm Michael." I said, and I extended out my hand. She shook it and replied, "I'm Indigo." I replied, "Indigo? That's an interesting name." She responded, "My father was an interesting man." At that moment, I knew there was something special about her. We both finally made it out of the poetry club, and we started to go our separate ways, but once I was outside, my senses started to go crazy; there were so many voices at once and so many images it felt like my head was splitting.

I'm not sure what triggered it, but I couldn't control it until I looked across the street, and everything quickly stopped, and there she was. I couldn't believe my eyes because it's been so long, but I saw Vanessa. Once again, you would think being a vampire, you would lose your emotional side, but here I am, going into a ridiculous frenzy with so many different feelings. She was heading in the same direction I was, so I followed her stealthily. I just could not believe my eyes.

It's been two years since I was turned, and I'm just now seeing Vanessa. I was excited and nervous. I followed her to this coffee shop, and from the looks of it, it seemed as if she was waiting to meet someone;

now I was trying to figure out if I should approach her or remain just a memory, and then I saw Derek walking into the shop, and they greeted each other with a warm embrace as if they were together, I wasn't sure.

Still, nonetheless, I became angry, and the more I watched them together, the angrier I became. I had no choice but to leave the area and return to Aries's mansion. When I returned, I demanded that Aries explain himself. "I want my old life back," I said. Aries replied, "What are you talking about." "Fix this, reverse it. Change me back, human now." I said. Aries said, "You sound ridiculous; you can't just pick and choose when you want to be a vampire. It doesn't work like that." His response upset me even more, "Why did you do this to me?" I said. Aries laughed and replied, "I Gave you a gift; why are you upset little puppy."

He patted me on the head. I pushed his hand away and asked, "Why did you take my life away? Why did you choose me! WHY ME?!" Aries then stood up and shouted, "ENOUGH! I'm not sure why you are upset, nor do I care; I'm not sure who you think you're dealing with, but one thing I do know you better correct yourself before I do." Aries's words didn't do anything but enrage me more, and it made him angry that I was not moved by his threat, so he struck me, sending me into the wall.

I then warped in front of him, and he grabbed me by my neck. As I struggled, he got closer and said, "Calm down, little Mikey, you won't win this one." My eyes turned yellow; my strength increased, but it was still not enough to take Aries on. We went back and forth, punching and slashing each other, but after being tossed around like a rag doll, I was fatigued, and Aries grew tired of all the fighting.

He yelled, "I'VE HAD ENOUGH OF THIS!" He broke the leg off a wooden chair and slowly approached me. I thought I was ready for his next attack until the fog appeared, and I could no longer see him, nor could I sense him; he then grabbed me and pierced my heart with the broken wood from the chair. It felt like the wind got knocked out of me, and Aries said, "Face it, Michael, you will need an army to beat me... You are what you are, and it is no! Taking it back... I could kill you all over again, but you won't come back this time!"

Aries threw me to the ground and continued, "There's not enough room for both of us in this town..." As soon as the fog cleared, he disappeared, and that was the last time I saw Aries. It took some time to heal from the injuries I received during that fight. It took almost a full week to get all my strength back. After the fight, I found myself wandering the hallways of the home Aries built. I tried to shake my obsession with this "Vampire Journal." Still, every time I walked by the library, those memories of Aries's past would be triggered, so I decided to avoid the library altogether and focus on other things.

Three years have passed since that night, and every moment from then replays in my head constantly, and the more I relive those moments, the more my hatred for Aries grows. To distract myself from those thoughts, I learned to blend in with the crowd and try to appear as normal to people as possible; I have even gone on dates with Indigo, the girl I met at that poetry club.

We hit it off instantly and had been seeing each other a lot, and I started to feel some sort of connection there; I was not sure if I wanted to let her keep her life or take it or possibly turn her into what I am, the more I thought about it, she would make an exceptional vampire.

# Chapter Four

# **Another Chance**

I never stopped loving Vanessa, but due to my current situation, I told myself I had to let her go, and seeing her that night changed everything. I'm not sure if I could even speak to her or what I would say or do if she and I were ever face to face again; I mean, what could she possibly have to say to her boyfriend, who's been dead for five years and even though I'm a monster could she still love me? Would she want to be like me? Do I even have the courage to make her like me?

The answer to all those questions is no, and even though I miss her, it would be wise to stay away from her. Seeing Indigo every week was a good distraction for me. She was an interesting girl, a law school student without a care in the world. Being with her was like an escape from everything; well, my world.

We were on what seemed to be our 7th date, and at the end of each one, I would walk her home and kiss her forehead before parting ways. That night was different; she stopped me from leaving and invited me into her home, which surprised me because I was not expecting that. "Stay the night with me." She said, I smiled and said, "As you wish." We entered her home, and she said, "Wait here." She then went to her bedroom. 10 minutes passed, and I heard, "Michael, come here." I gladly followed her instructions, and there she was waiting for me on her bed, looking just as beautiful as ever, the real definition of perfection.

She slowly approached me and started removing my clothes, starting with my shirt, my belt, and then my pants. She then whispered gently, "I don't bite." I pulled her closer, looked her in her eyes, and replied, "But I do." The way she was smiling at me you would think I had her in a trance, she started kissing me passionately. We began making love, and with each position, everything intensified; her moan was simply beautiful and it drew me closer to her.

She would lose herself with every stroke and beg me for more, gripping my shoulders and slowly clawing at my back. With each moan, the monster in me grew larger; she looked me in the eyes and said, "I'm yours…yours forever." Her body began to shake as if she was about to explode. She then released a moan loud enough to wake her neighbors; by this time, I could no longer contain myself. I had no control, and it was impossible to keep it together.

I bit her, and that sweet, beautiful moan quickly turned into a soft scream. She tried to push me off, but it was too late. My bite already consumed her. I unhooked my fangs from her neck and went to the bathroom to wash the blood off my face; I got dressed and then made my way to the living room to wait. After sitting in her living room for nearly two hours, flipping through channels, I suddenly heard a scream. I quickly warped to her bedroom; she was standing there puzzled.

She was so confused she looked lost; of course, she would be confused as to why she is waking up and finding herself covered in blood. "Indigo?" I said. She then looked at me and screamed, "WHAT THE HELL DID YOU DO TO ME!!!!" I replied, "Calm down, everything will make sense after a while, but first, how do you feel?" She looked around the room, glanced at the bed, and saw the blood stains covering her sheets, she placed her left hand on her neck where I bit her, now she's looking at her hand and it's covered in blood. She turned to me, grabbed me, and said, "What is this? Why is my head splitting, and why am I so hungry."

I replied, "Indigo, listen to me, you're a vampire." [Indigo was in complete disbelief] "I made you what I am." "What?" she said. I replied,

"I made you unique and I can show you just how unique you are." I took her by the hand, helped her clean herself up, and we went into town. I began to teach her, and I must say she was a fast learner. She didn't need me to teach her much of anything. She took to her new life very well. She became a master of her vampire skills in a matter of days.

I was impressed; because what took me months to master only took her a few days. After a while, I let Indigo have her own unsupervised fun for once and I decided to take a small stroll down memory lane. After so many years passed by, you would think that being in front of Club Reign would not be so difficult for me, but let's be clear: I'm only here for one thing and one thing only. I made my way through the crowd, searching for a beautiful woman who could hold a conversation.

Our parents told us not to play with our food, but those days are long gone. As I am looking, I hear my name being called. Someone is trying to get my attention, but I didn't know who "Michael!!" I turned around, and to my surprise it was Derek. "Michael, oh my god!" He grabbed me and hugged me tight. "I can't believe it's really you; where have you been!" he said. I replied, "Derek, it has been a long time, hasn't it." Derek says, "Yeah, try five years. Man, you're supposed to be dead! Where have you been hiding?" I replied, "It's a long story, and someday I will." Derek cut me off and said, "Wait a minute, Vanessa's here!" Those words struck so much fear in me as if I was a helpless child, I wasn't sure what to do then; he called her over to us. "Vanessa! VANESSA!" he shouted.

She approached, and Derek said, "You'll never believe who's here." He turned and said, "Hey Mike…" When Derek turned around, I was gone. I quickly disappeared I was not yet ready to face Vanessa. The club ended, and everyone made their way out; I was sitting on top of a building across the street, watching Vanessa as she walked out and headed in my direction. "She's pretty," from the shadows Indigo said, "I didn't know you were here." I replied, "I bet she tastes as good as she looks." Indigo said, "You'll never know; now leave," I replied.

Vanessa made her way through the alley, Indigo quickly swept down and pinned Vanessa to a wall. "Hello, beautiful." Indigo snarled as she was about to strike; I then warped down to them, pushed Indigo into a wall, and said, "Are you hard of hearing? I said SHE'S OFF LIMITS!" Indigo looked at me confused and quickly warped away from the area, "Michael...?" Vanessa said. I slowly turned to her, and we sat there staring at each other, completely speechless, she was looking at me as if she was seeing a ghost.

# Chapter Five

# <u>The Vampire Journal</u>

I turned to walk away, but then Vanessa stopped me and said, "It's been five years; where have you been… all this time?" I replied, "It's a long story, and I'm unsure where to begin." It started to rain. Vanessa said, "Come with me; you need to know something." She called a cab, and we headed to her place. I was unsure of what she had to show me, but I knew reuniting with her at that moment felt so right.

We arrived at her home, and an elderly woman opened the door and said, "She's asleep; since you're home, I'm going to leave for the night." Vanessa said goodnight to the woman and closed the door. We went to the living room and sat down; there was an awkward silence for a moment, and then Vanessa said, "What was that back there? And where did you come from? You pushed that girl into a brick wall.

Was she after me or something? Who is she?" I said, "It's so many things I want to say and need to say, but I don't know how to explain it; I don't even know where to begin." Vanessa replied, "Well, you need to start somewhere; why did you leave me? Can you explain that? The doctors told us you were DEAD...and now you just show up out of nowhere. WHAT HAPPENED TO YOU!" I replied, "I DID DIE! I'm dead now and had no choice but to leave you." Then a tiny voice said, "Mommy?"

It was a little girl; she was the prettiest thing my eyes had ever seen. Vanessa said, "Sorry baby, did I wake you?" The little girl said, "Yes," and stared at me. Vanessa says, "Kendi say hello. Kendi says, "Hello," and then smiles so big. Vanessa said, "Say hello to your daughter, Michael." Kendi and I were both standing there looking at each other. I kneeled, and Kendi approached me and then hugged me. I kissed her forehead, and Vanessa said, "Okay, sweetie, time for bed." Kendi walks back toward her room, but first, she looks back and says, "Goodnight, Mommy."

I looked at Vanessa and said, "I had no idea; why didn't you tell me?" Vanessa said, "I was going to tell you after we celebrated at the club that night; why do you think I wasn't drinking any alcohol." We both laughed. I looked at my watch and realized it was time to go. "Vanessa, I have to leave, but I'll be back very soon, and I promise I can explain everything. I'm just out of time right now." "Come back tomorrow," Vanessa said. I hugged her, and then I left.

I returned home, threw my jacket over a chair, and there was Indigo. "So, who is she?" Indigo said. I replied, "She's none of your concern." Indigo said, "She must be pretty special for you to throw me around like that." I said, "Indigo, enough; I told you she was off limits, and you ignored me. I won't apologize for what I did. Now leave it alone." I walked away and started heading toward my bedroom. As I walked by the library, that memory of the journal was triggered yet again; this only happens when I walk by the library.

I had never been inside this library before, but my gut told me to go in; once inside, I started searching the shelves, removing books one by one. I kept making my way through the library, and as I continued to explore, that memory would get stronger and stronger; I was not sure what it meant, but I knew I needed to keep looking. 25 minutes had gone by, and I was still coming up empty-handed; I finally made my way to the last shelf, and as I approached, the memory had become so strong that it overpowered me, strong enough that I could see what Aries was doing and where he was hiding it.

He hid it in a wall behind the shelves. I searched for that exact location, and I found it. The wall was weak, weak enough to punch through, so I did just that. Once the dust cleared, I was able to pull the journal out. I wasn't sure why I needed to find it or why those memories drew me to it, but it must be a reason. I sat in my room reading the journal, which held so many vampire secrets Aries was not ready to share with me. It spoke about our different skills and how to master them.

It also spoke about how we were created and how Dracula was the first. I was so amazed by all the things I didn't know, and in a matter of minutes, I obtained so much knowledge it was crazy; I decided to put the journal down and get some rest because I still had to explain all of this to Vanessa tomorrow night. As soon as the sun set, I quickly got dressed and made my way back over to Vanessa's house, but when I arrived, something was off; the energy I felt was alarming to me.

I felt rage from someone in the house, but I wasn't sure who it was, so I quickly knocked on the door and heard, "You need to leave! Stop coming here unannounced." Vanessa opened the door, and Derek came out and he looked pissed, so I asked, "Is everything okay?" Vanessa replies, "Oh, Michael, yes, everything is fine. Derek was just leaving." I could tell the energy was disturbed, so I tried to lighten the mood. "The three of us are back together again after all these years.

I don't know about you two, but I love reunions." Derek didn't seem amused and walked past me without saying a word, so I followed him, "Hey Derek, is everything okay? You good?" Derek looked at me as if he was disgusted and said, "These last few years have been great, and suddenly, things shift. Who gave you the right to abandon her and try to come back into her life after so long." The question Derek asked made me realize that the problem he had was with me; I replied, "I'm not sure what's going on with you, but I had a good reason to leave, but I'm back, and I'm back for good so whatever anger you feel towards me you need to get over it and soon, or I'll gladly help you."

I walked away and went inside. "What was that about?" I asked Vanessa, and she replied, "Nothing. Derek is upset about things not going his way, as always. So anyway, I hope you can give me some answers about what happened." I stood there like a deer in headlights, but I knew I had to explain things to her, "Yes," I replied, "I have a lot to say, and what I have to say just might alter everything between us, but you deserve to know the truth." Vanessa sat on the couch, and I knew it was time to reveal my secret.

"Vanessa, I'm not the same Michael anymore; I'm something else, something worse." Vanessa replied, "What do you mean?" I took a deep breath and said, "I'm a vampire." Vanessa looked at me with so much confusion, and for a moment, there was complete silence, and then Vanessa shouted, "WHAT?!" as if she were in disbelief. "I'm serious. Just hear me out. That night in the alley, that man bit me; I was rushed to the hospital with severe puncture wounds on my neck, and hours later, I was pronounced dead."

Vanessa had this look on her face as if she somewhat believed what I was saying, but a part of her could not accept it; I continued. "The man who bit me, his name is Aries, and I've been gone all these years because I was learning how to deal with this new version of me, and I didn't think to seek you or Derek out because I wasn't sure of what would happen so I stayed away and then one day I seen you and I was hypnotized I knew I couldn't stay away any longer."

With her mouth open, Vanessa was sitting on the couch and said, "So you're a vampire. Like an actual vampire." I replied, "Yes, I know this is a lot to take in." Vanessa cut me off and began to laugh. I said, "What's funny?" she replied, "You came over tonight to tell me this bull shit, like really?! Michael, this isn't funny, and you sound ignorant; you said you would explain everything, and you're turning this into a childish joke. Maybe you should leave and stay gone this time. Call me when you grow up."

"Grow Up?!" I replied, "I'm here because you deserve the truth, but words aren't what you need. I need to show you proof." I stood back and shifted into predator mode; my eyes began to glow, and my teeth began to grow. Vanessa stood up in shock, backing away and heading towards the kitchen. She turned around quickly, and there I was, right behind her. "You see! This isn't a game. I'm a monster now!" My teeth and eyes returned to normal, and I said, "But I will never hurt you or

Kendi; I'll protect you guys, I promise. I'll leave now, but you deserved to know the truth."

As I began to walk toward the door, Vanessa stopped me. "Michael, wait!" she said, then she came up to me, hugged me, and said, "I'm sorry this happened to you, and I'm sorry I didn't believe you." I replied, "You have nothing to be sorry about; just know I'm doing everything I can to change back to normal." Vanessa hugged me and said, "I love you, Michael; until you return to normal, promise me, you'll come to see us every night."

I looked at Vanessa and said, "I promise." She kissed me, and then I left. I returned home and continued to read the vampire journal, hoping I would obtain some secrets about possibly returning human or how to be this and be with someone who isn't like this. As I continued to read and fill my head with more vampire knowledge, I discovered the most important page in this book. It reads, "Although being a vampire isn't for everyone, and most will either regret this choice or maybe a choice wasn't given to you, but if you want the option of being human again, then you must kill the one who made you."

# Chapter Six

# **<u>Exposed</u>**

After all this time, Michael finally found the answer he was looking for, "Kill the one who made you," is what the book said, and at that moment, Michael knew if he were ever to return to his human form, he would need to find Aries and kill him. As Michael continued to read the journal, it also stated, "Killing the one who made you will turn all of your undead servants back to their human form as well."

Michael jumped out of bed excitedly and called for Indigo, "Indigo!" Michael shouted, "Indigo! Come here!" Indigo quickly warped to Michael and said, "What is it? Are you OK?" Michael replied, "Answer this: Do you miss your old life? Do you miss being human? Do you miss your family?" Indigo replied, "Yes, I miss everything, but mostly the sun." Michael quickly replied, "What if I told you we may have an opportunity to regain our old lives? Would you be interested?" Indigo said, "How?" Michael showed her the vampire journal and the page on how to turn back human. Indigo looks at Michael and says, "So what do we do?" Michael replies, "We find Aries and kill him, but we can't do it alone.

I fought him once before, and I couldn't beat him; even with the strength I have now, I am still no match; we'll need some help." Indigo says, "What kind of help?" Michael turns to Indigo, grins, and says, "After my fight with Aries, he told me, and I quote, you will need an army to defeat me, so let's go get an army." Creating an army means recruiting individuals to join your team, but before Michael could scout for new talent, he had to share his newfound discovery with Vanessa; the following night, Michael paid Vanessa a visit. Michael arrived at Vanessa's home, and he rang the doorbell.

Vanessa answered the door, and she knew something was up because Michael had this look of pure excitement as if he were a kid on Christmas day, ready to open gifts. "What's with the look?" Vanessa says, "I'm just happy to see you, is all I promise. Can I come in?" Michael replies. "Of course." Vanessa says. Kendi was playing with her toys in the living room. Michael waves at her; instead of waving back, Kendi grabs her toys and goes to her bedroom. "Sorry, it's going to take some time getting used to you," Vanessa says.

Michael replies, "Trust me, I understand; I'm still trying to get used to this." they laugh. Michael continues, "So I have something to share with you, but first, I have a question. Since revealing what I am to you, does it make you nervous? Or scared?" Vanessa chuckles and replies, "Surprisingly, no, I guess I'm still in shock at the fact that you're still alive. I didn't have time to concern myself with anything else."

Michael is relieved by Vanessa's response and smiles; Vanessa continues, "How is this whole thing supposed to work? You know, with you being a vampire." With a huge grin, Michael replies, "For starters, I will never harm you or Kendi; I will protect you both no matter the cost and lastly, I might not be a vampire forever." Vanessa turned to Michael with a shocked and confused look on her face and said, "What did you say?" Michael says, "I have this journal, and it says."

In mid-sentence, Michael paused and looked at the door because something triggered his senses. Vanessa says, "What? What is it?" Michael says, "Derek is here, and he's pissed." Then there was a hard knock on the door, another one, and another one. Finally, Vanessa answered. When she opened it, Derek barged right in; he appeared drunk. Vanessa says, "Derek, I told you not to come here unannounced."

A drunk Derek turns to Vanessa and says, "Am I not good enough for you?! For five years, you cried about Michael. Michael this, Michael that, and you finally come to terms with his death." Vanessa replies, "Derek, you're drunk. I'm calling you a cab." Derek replies, "I am not finished. He has been gone for FIVE YEARS! He can't just come back as if nothing has happened; I've been there for you and Kendi."

Michael felt Derek getting more and more angry as he spoke. Michael said, "Derek, I know my timing isn't perfect, and you might have had feelings for Vanessa, but I'm here now, and as I said before, you need to get with the program." Vanessa says, "Michael, it's OK. I called him a cab; Derek is leaving." Now angry, Derek walks to Vanessa, pushes her, and yells, "DID I ASK YOU TO CALL A CAB? I HAVE SOMETHING TO SAY & YOU ARE GOING TO LISTEN!"

Michael quickly warps to Derek and pins him against the wall, his eyes glowing yellow and his fangs showing. Michael then snarls at Derek as if he were an angry tiger. Michael says, "Because you are drunk, I won't hurt you, but if you ever come near my family again, I will kill you slowly; this friendship no longer exists, now leave us alone!"

In shock about what he has just seen, Derek says, "Michael, your eyes." Michael releases Derek; Vanessa opens the door and says, "Derek, your cab is here." Derek slowly walks toward the door; every few steps, he looks at Michael in total shock at what he just witnessed. As Derek reaches the front door and prepares to exit, he turns to Michael one last time and says, "What happened to you?" Michael does not answer; he gives Derek an evil glare as he exits Vanessa's home. Vanessa shuts her front door and turns around to look at Michael; Michael says, "I'm sorry." Vanessa replies, "It's OK, now Derek knows."

They both begin to laugh and then Vanessa says, "So what were you going to say before he showed up. You have a journal?" Michael quickly pulls out the journal to show Vanessa; Michael says, "Yes! Here it is, it is called The Vampire Journal, and it holds many vampire secrets. The one who made me tried to hide this. I'm unsure why, but I found it." Michael turns to the final page of the journal and says, "Here, read this." Vanessa reads and then looks up to Michael and says, "You can turn back human? How do we know this is even true?" Michael replies,

"We don't, but we have to find out; it says that killing the one who made you will turn you back, and any vampire servants you may have will also return to their human form." Vanessa says, "OK, so what now?" Michael says, "I must find the one who made me.

It won't be easy, but Indigo and I are working on a plan." Vanessa gives Michael the side eye and says, "Who is Indigo?" Michael replies, "The girl I shoved away from you a few nights ago." Vanessa says, "Oh, she's Indigo now; she has a name now." Michael laughs and replies, "She's always had a name. We just never talked about it." Vanessa rolled her eyes, and Michael said, "Look, we're getting off-topic; the plan is to go out and recruit maybe one or two people to join us and search for Aries and then kill him." Vanessa says, "Who is Aries?" Michael replies, "Aries is the one who bit me and turned me into this."

# Chapter Seven

# Recruiting Season

Michael and Indigo are discussing their plan for who they will recruit to join their mission in defeating Aries. "We need to be smart about this because everyone isn't fit to handle this type of power." Michael says, [continues] "Starting tonight, we can scowl the city in search of recruits. Whoever you find, bring them here, and I'll turn them." Indigo says, "How do we know where to look?" Michael says, "Follow your intuition, let that be your guide, and trust it." Weeks have gone by, and Michael and Indigo have yet to be successful, night after night, with no luck.

In the meantime, Derek has been doing his own research, working tirelessly, trying to figure out what his former best friend has become. "I was drunk, but I know what I saw." said Derek, thinking out loud. "Sharp teeth, glowing eyes. What happened to you, Michael?" Derek has been searching for weeks, trying to figure out what exactly has happened to Michael; he stumbled across a website specializing in monster findings. The website contains several articles about different types of supernatural monsters that could be roaming the world, some fiction, and some facts.

Derek comes across an article titled "Vampyr." The article describes what a Vampire is. After reading several articles about this topic, Derek believes he has discovered what Michael is. "He's a vampire," Derek said to himself in a shocking tone. "He'll kill Vanessa if provoked; I must stop him before it's too late." While Michael and Indigo continue their search for recruits, Derek begins to do his own recruiting. After weeks of research, separating facts from fiction as best he could, Derek began to promote an upcoming presentation about his recent discovery.

As Michael and Indigo continue searching for recruits, the duo comes across a flyer that reads, "Want to stop living in fear? Text the number below and join me at a secret location to determine how to win this war." At the bottom, it reads Organized by Derek Graham. Michael laughs and mumbles, "I should've killed him." Indigo replies, "You know who he is? What is this?" Michael replies, "I knew him… It's nothing to worry about; we've got other things to focus on right now." Michael and Indigo decide to split up and continue their search. Indigo notices a huge crowd gathering by the local college, so she follows.

Michael continues to wander around town; he then stumbles across a beautiful woman, 5'7, with cinnamon skin and long silky hair; she's painting a portrait of a couple. Michael admires her artwork; as he runs his fingers through each painting on her display, she looks at Michael and says, "May I help you?" Michael replies, "Such talent." the woman says, "Thank you. Hi, I'm Jasmine."

Michael replies, "Hello, my name is Michael." Michael then kisses her hand and says, "It's a pleasure to meet you." The two of them gaze into each other's eyes for a moment, then Michael says, "That accent, you're not from here, are you?" Jasmine says, "I was raised in the Philippines." Michael says, "The Philippines, see, I had everything wrong. Judging by the way you look; I would've guessed you were from Brazil." Jasmine smiles at Michael and says, "No, my father is from here; he's African American. My mother is 100% Filipino." Michael smiles back at Jasmine and says, "Well, whatever the demographic, you're absolutely gorgeous." [Michael continues] "So, do you have any more artwork, or is everything on display?" Jasmine smiles at Michael and says, "I have more, but I only brought what would fit in my car." Michael replies, "Oh, okay."

With a slight stutter, Jasmine says, "Since I'm done for the night, how about you come with me to my apartment, and I can show you all of my artwork." Michael grins at Jasmine and says, "You lead the way." Back at the college, Indigo stumbles across what seems to be a seminar. She quietly finds herself a seat, and as she pretends to be interested in the presentation that's about to take place, her eyes start to wander, and she begins to scout the room for a potential recruit.

The announcer walked onto the stage, grabbed the mic, and said, "Thank you, everyone, for coming, and now I bring you the man of the hour. Please, everyone, give a warm welcome to our guest speaker, Mr. Derek Graham!" the audience began to applaud; Indigo quickly locked eyes at the stage once she heard Derek's name thinking to herself "this is the man Michael knows from the flyer." With a tremble in his voice, Derek begins his presentation on "Winning the war against vampires." As Derek continues, people start to make their way toward the exit; as he pleads his case, Indigo believes she has found someone worth recruiting, a young college student who seems unimpressed with Derek's presentation. The young man also starts to make his way toward the exit, and Indigo follows.

"Well, that was fun." Indigo says, and the young man turns around. "Yeah, fun and weird." The young man replied, he and Indigo began to chuckle, "So, did you believe anything he was saying back there?" Indigo said. The young man replied, "What about vampires? Of course not." As they continued to walk, the young man said, "I'm Jeremy, by the way." With a big smile, Indigo replied, "Nice to meet you, Jeremy; my name is Indigo."

The two shake hands and make their way toward the exit from the building; Jeremy continues the conversation. "That presentation was interesting, huh?" Indigo replies. "I wasn't paying that much attention; I was too busy focused on you." Jeremy begins to smile and says, "I've never seen you around campus before. Are you new?" Indigo replies, "Just transferred." Jeremy says, "Well, welcome to our school. I wish I noticed you from the beginning; all that talks about vampires' kind of threw me off." They laughed, and then Jeremy said, "It's pretty late; let me walk you home, to your dorm, or wherever you live." Indigo says, "I would like that." Jeremy starts to walk Indigo "home".

Meanwhile, Michael is looking through more of Jasmine's artwork back at her apartment. "You're really talented." Michael says. Jasmine replies, "Thank you so much; it's hard to make any money when nobody notices you or your hard work." Michael begins to stare at Jasmine and smiles; he says, "What are you afraid of?" With a perplexed look, Jasmine replies, "I don't like spiders, mice, maybe." Michael says, "What about people? Do people in the world scare you?" Jasmine now looking at Michael, trying to figure out the point he's trying to make. She replies, "I guess, truthfully, I'm not sure what you're trying to ask me." Michael stands up slowly and says, "I'll get right to the point. I'm in the middle of a crucial task and looking for assistance; you seem to be a perfect recruit for this task."

Jasmine looks at Michael and seems to be very much intrigued. Back at the school, Derek appears stressed out and disappointed by the people who attended his seminar; they laughed at him and walked out in the middle of his presentation. Derek is cleaning up his display and packing his things. A voice from what was supposed to be an empty theater yells out, "I believe you!" Derek turns around to see who said that. He was then approached by five men who looked like hunters.

Each one with a trucker hat, different color flannels on; they looked ready to take on the toughest predators in the world. The men met Derek on the stage, and one man repeated, "I believe you." Derek replies, "Is this a joke? Or are you serious? What makes you believe me?" the man introduces himself. "My name is John Pearson, and I've seen the supernatural things you discussed in your presentation." With a huge grin, Derek replies, "Well, Mr. Pearson, I've also seen things. Let me buy you and your colleagues a drink, and let's discuss the things we've seen and how we can destroy them."

Chapter Eight

# <u>Welcome to the Family</u>

T he sound of loud footsteps is coming from down the hall, grunting sounds coming from both Jeremy and Jasmine as they begin to wake up. Indigo is sitting in a chair, filing her nails, and whistling; Jeremy and Jasmine look at each other with confusion; the footsteps grow louder by the second. Indigo stands up as Michael enters the room; Indigo says, "We've been waiting for you." Michael smiles at Indigo, winks, and says, "I welcome you with open arms; now I know there's a lot of confusion about why you're here & about what is going on, and you may have some questions." Before Michael could continue, Jeremy interrupted his speech and said, "Why do I feel so weird?" Michael smirks and says, "Well, if you allow me to finish, I can explain everything."

Michael tries to continue, and Jeremy interrupts his speech a second time and says, "Why are we here? And why do I feel like you've done something to us." Michael appears annoyed as he stares at Jeremy and says, "Well, Jeremy, let's get straight to the point, but if you interrupt me again, I'll see to it that you have no more breath in your body." Jeremy looks at Michael with fear in his eyes, knowing that now is the perfect time to bite his tongue. Michael continues, "I've given you all what is called the dark gift; it's temporary but necessary for the time being.

The truth of the matter is I need your help." Jasmine begins to quiver uncontrollably; Jeremy looks at Michael and says, "Help with what?"

32

Michael responds, "I have recruited you two to help me complete an impossible task I can't accomplish alone." Jasmine says, "What task is that." Michael says, "To kill the vampire that made me." Both Jasmine and Jeremy looked at each other with confusion and hesitantly laughed. Jeremy mumbled, "A vampire." Jeremy then turns from Jasmine, looks at Indigo, and flares his nose "So much for believing in vampires huh" Jeremey says.

Indigo is refusing to make eye contact with Jeremy. A now angry Jeremy turns to Michael and says, "You called it a gift, what?" Michael interrupts Jeremy and Says, "Yes, a gift, welcome to your new life." Jeremy quickly responds, "This isn't a gift; whatever it is, it's a CURSE!" Michael angrily says, "Well then, WELCOME TO HELL MOTHERFUCKER!" Michael then warps to Jeremy and continues, "Make no mistake, this evil is necessary for the time being! And you will do what needs to be done. Your lives are mine until I have no further use for them; now die!" Jeremy and Jasmine grunt in agony as their human bodies begin to die out so their undead souls can take over.

Standing over Jeremy, Michael kneels and says, "Never question me again; as I said before, this is temporary. Help me, and everything goes back to normal." Michael stands up and approaches Jasmine; Michael kneels and kisses Jasmine on the forehead and then exits the room. Indigo frowns at Jasmine and glares angrily at Michael as he exits. Over five months, the tension between Michael and Jeremy has died down; though Jeremy doesn't approve of what he's become or Michael's "Mission," he's willing to be a team player and help with this current task so he can be done with it.

Jeremy returns to the mansion after a night of hunting with Indigo; he walks past the library, where he notices Michael is standing there and appears as if he were brooding. Jeremy approaches Michael and says, "Hey, Michael. Can I ask you a question?" Michael responds, "Sure, what is it?" Jeremy says, "Why is this mission so important to you? You didn't exactly tell us all the details of this "task" we are supposed to help you with." Michael takes a deep breath and says, "I had a life before all of this; it was beautiful, it wasn't perfect, but it was mine, and one night it was taken away from me. I know you had a life before this as well. The only difference is I plan to give it back to you."

Michael sat down and continued, "When I became this primal animal, I decided to take control and own it, or at least try to. Then I discovered the life taken from me had new meaning, and I want it back; to do so, I must kill the one who made me. I failed the first time, but now that I outnumber him, I believe we can do it." Jeremy feels sorry for Michael and says, "I'm sorry."

Michael continues, "I know you're not a fan of what you are but believe me when I say it won't last much longer." Michael stands up, and before exiting the library, he turns to Jeremy and says, "Once he is dead, everything goes back to normal." As Michael exits, Jeremy says, "You have our support." Michael smiles as he exits the room.

The following night, Michael is getting ready for his nightly routine of feeding and going to see Vanessa and Kendi. Still, before he can exit the mansion, he hears, "Where do you go every night?" from the top of the stairs. Michael turns around and sees Jasmine walking down the stairs. Michael replies, "There are some things about me you don't need to know." Jasmine makes her way down the stairs and says, "I never see you is all." Jasmine slowly approaches Michael and tries to win him over by being seductive. "Is there something you need, Jasmine?" Michael says.

Jasmine responds, "How about we stay in tonight? I can." Michael quickly interrupts Jasmine and says, "Jasmine, I hope you're not asking me for my time because I am fresh out." Michael turns back towards the front door and leaves. Jasmine hears from the top of the stairs, "He's not all that bad, you know." Jasmine turns around, and from the shadows, Jeremy appears and continues, "He's just not into you." Jasmine scoffs at Jeremy and says, "What do you know about what or who he's into?" Jeremy walks down the stairs, approaches Jasmine, and says, "I just know from watching that performance that he's not interested."

Jasmine replies, "Oh, so what, he's into you?" Jeremy laughs loudly, saying, "Don't make it weird, but no, he's just focused on other things." From the mansion's west wing, Indigo approaches Jeremy and Jasmine and says, "Michael's focus is none of your concern; now, how about the two of you focus on your feeding tonight." Jasmine flares her nose up at Indigo.

Indigo then looks at Jasmine as if she's trying to challenge her, and Jeremy says, "We're actually on our way out now." Jeremy grabs Jasmine by the arm and escorts her out of the mansion. Jeremy says to Jasmine outside, "Why are you always trying to challenge her!" Jasmine replies, "Because I think it's time someone knocks her off her high horse." Jeremy says, "She's not even trying to compete. Only you are." Jasmine scoffs at Jeremy again and says, "Whatever, come on, let's go." With a confused look, Jeremy says, "Where exactly are we going?" Jasmine says, "Feeding, remember."

Back in town, Michael is at an Italian restaurant enjoying an evening of live music and wine with Vanessa accompanying him. Michael and Vanessa are smiling at each other as if they're back in high school and on their first date, "Dance with me." Michael says. Smiling like she won the lottery, Vanessa quickly takes Michael by the hand and guides him to the dance floor. "So, when are you going to finally come home?" Vanessa says, "Come home?" Michael replies, and Vanessa says, "Yeah, permanently, with me and Kendi." Michael looks at Vanessa with slight confusion and says, "You want me to move in? Even though I'm still this?" Vanessa replies, "You seem to have a lock on it, right? Kendi constantly asks to see her dad but also asks why she can only see you at night."

Michael releases a sigh and takes Vanessa by the hand, and the two of them return to their seats. Michael turns to Vanessa, saying, "Moving in isn't a good idea right now." Vanessa interrupts Michael, saying, "Why? Kendi really wants to know you better." Michael quickly responds, "If I move in, she will still only be able to see me at night...

listen, I am very close to ending this. You're just going to have to be patient and trust me."

Vanessa now frowning, with a look of disappointment; after three minutes of silent treatment, Michael looks at Vanessa, and before he can begin, he senses an unwanted presence and quickly becomes irritated. Michael turns to Vanessa and says, "Come on, it's time to go." Vanessa looks at Michael and says, "Why?" Michael quickly replies, "I have to get going, is all." Vanessa gathers her belongings, and the two end their date early, Michael walks Vanessa home. The two arrive at Vanessa's home; Michael walks her to the door.

Michael tries to kiss Vanessa, but she turns her head and opens the door. Before closing the door behind her, Michael says, "The two of you won't have to wait much longer; I promise you that." Vanessa smiles at Michael and shuts the door. Michael turns around and begins to walk down the steps. He turns left and makes his way further down the block. Michael knows he's being followed and is purposely luring whomever away from Vanessa's home.

He makes his way to this abandoned parking structure. He suddenly stops and says, "You honestly think following me is safe?" From the shadows appear, Jeremy and Jasmine, the two slowly approach Michael. "I saw the two of you back in town while I was at the restaurant; sneaking around just isn't your thing; maybe we should work on that." Jasmine scoffs and says, "So this is your idea of hunting alone?" Michael replies, "This is my idea of it being my business and not yours; why are the two of you here!" Jeremy looks at both Michael and Jasmine, refusing to say anything. Jasmine says, "So, who is she." Michael looked at Jasmine with pure hate in his eyes. Jasmine says, "Hello! Who is she, and why is she a secret? WHAT MAKES HER SO SPECIAL."

Jeremy tries to calm Jasmine down and tells her they should go. "No! Don't touch me! He owes us an explanation." Michael smirks and says, "Us? Or You? Quite frankly, Jasmine, I don't owe either of you a fucking thing; now I advise you to head back home. The sun will be up soon." Michael turns around as if he's about to depart from Jasmine and Jeremy, but then Jasmine quickly warps in front of Michael, trying to stop him from leaving. "You're in my way." Michael said.

Jasmine quickly replied, "You chose me for a reason. Am I right, or am I wrong?" Michael says, "As I said before, Jasmine, I chose you to help me with a task." Jasmine says, "So that's it, I'm a gun for hire." Quickly, Michael says, "Basically...What do you think this is?" Jasmine replies, "You chose me! What do I have to do for you to notice me? Kill your secret lover back at that house because I will!"

Jasmine attempts to warp, but Michael quickly interrupts her by warping in front of her and grabbing Jasmine by the throat; now Michael is angry and gripping Jasmine's neck tighter and tighter and says, "If you think you're going to bring any sort of harm to her I might as well kill you right here." Michael lets go of Jasmine; she hits the ground hard, looks at Michael, and says, "Do you love her?" Michael says, "Why is that any of your concern?" Jasmine quickly stands up and shouts, "Because I Love you!" Michael shouts back, "You don't love me! You love the monster! You love the power you have; you don't love me, Jasmine; you're just confused."

Jasmine looks like her heart has just been shattered into pieces; she turns and runs the other way so fast that she disappears into the night. Jeremy says, "I'll go find her and calm her down." Michael is somewhat upset at himself for hurting Jasmine's feelings, but this is nothing more than a brief arrangement, and everyone will go their separate ways when it's all said and done.

# Chapter Nine

# **Hunting Season**

Derek and his team have been preparing to kill his used-to-be best friend, Michael, for months. Clint is in the target practice room, letting off a few rounds while Todd cleans and polishes their weapons. Meanwhile, Derek is staring at an old picture of himself, Vanessa, and Michael. As Derek stares at the picture, Teddrick approaches and says, "We're all good to go, boss man, just waiting for John to get back, and if he brings us some good Intel, then we can move on with the next phase of our plan."

Derek sits silently and continues to stare at his friends' picture; Teddrick says, "Hey Derek, did you hear me?" Still not a peep from Derek, Teddrick turns around to make his exit out of the room. Derek says, "What made you join this "movement" Teddrick?" Teddrick turns to Derek, saying, "I have a personal interest in this movement." Derek replies, "What interest is that?" Teddrick grabs a chair and sits down to tell his story.

"A couple years ago, I came here to visit my sister; she had just graduated college with her master's degree, and she wanted to celebrate at this club called Club "Reign." Derek scoffs and says, "There's always something going on at that club." Teddrick continues, "Well, she was dancing with this guy; I wasn't going to interrupt because she was having a good time. I looked away for a moment, and she was gone; I figured she and the guy ran off to hook up or something.

When it was time to leave, I went to look for her, and when I found her, she was lifeless and extremely pale. The doctors said she didn't have an ounce of blood in her body, and that's when I knew something that wasn't from this earth took my sister." Derek says, "I am truly sorry to hear that; I have a similar story, except it involves my best friend. He was killed outside of Club Reign as well; he was not killed; he was injured. His girlfriend at the time and I rushed him to the hospital, where he later died from his injuries." Teddrick says, "Wow, man, I'm so sorry."

Derek continues, "But he didn't die; five years later, he shows back up in both of our lives, but he was different; he showed me just how different he was and that he was no longer my best friend; he is the monster who inspired this little movement of ours, and he is the one we are going to kill first" Teddrick replies "That's rough having your best friend involved, I wish people were more aware but its ok we'll make them see."

Those words sparked something in Derek: "We'll make them see, that's perfect!" Derek says. Teddrick looks at Derek with confusion and says, "What's perfect?" Derek just laughs as he quickly writes a new plan in his notebook. Derek then looks at Teddrick and says Let me know when John gets back, Teddrick says, "Sure thing," and walks off. Teddrick calls John for an update; John tells Teddrick, "I'm tracking two of them right now; I'll be in touch." John hangs the phone up and continues his mission; he's following two people, a man, and a woman, who fit the description of vampires. "The way they move, how they stand, it's just not normal." John said to himself. He followed the two of them to a high school.

He then flew a small drone above them and set them as targets on the drone so they could be tracked further and listened to. "Why are we at a school?" the man said, "Easy targets, you smell that? We can drain the janitor." The woman said. The two disappeared into the shadows, but the drone still had a good lock on them and proceeded to follow.

Inside is a young man who attends the school and a janitor wrapping up his shift while whistling and listening to music on the radio. The janitor is putting away his cleaning supplies. He sends a text to his son saying, "All finished down here; I'll be up in twenty minutes." The janitor locked his supply closet and looked over his checklist to ensure he didn't miss anything; with everything checked off, he made his way toward the door.

He reached for the door, which was locked; he tugged at it, even tried hitting it with his shoulder, but nothing. "How is it locked?" He said to himself. Out of nowhere, he heard a woman's laugh. He turned quickly to see if anyone was there but saw nothing. He turns back to the door to give it another try, and he then hears the woman's laugh again, which prompts him to turn around a second time.

This time, he doesn't see a woman. However, he did see a set of blue, glowing eyes, and from the shadows, the woman appeared. He noticed her sharp fangs and claws and a set of green glowing eyes behind her. A man appeared and stood behind her. The janitor quickly turns back to the door to try and escape the room; out of nowhere, John's drone picks up a loud scream within the school.

He quickly tries to pinpoint exactly where the scream came from to locate the victim. Due to frustration, Jeremy and Jasmine are unaware they're being tracked; Jasmine is still upset about Michael disregarding her feelings. Jeremy is focused on trying to keep Jasmine content because with the two of them being distracted, neither one of them is using their senses accurately.

Jasmine stops and says, "Do you hear that?" She turns to Jeremy with a sinister grin and says, "Someone else is here, a student." Jeremy, now annoyed, says, "A student? I don't think we're allowed to kill kids, Jas." Jasmine rolls her eyes and continues to follow the heartbeat she heard; Jeremy and Jasmine stumble across a young dark-haired male no more than sixteen years old who appears to be working on an assignment in his math class.

The two approach; Jasmine says, "Hello, cutie, what's your name?" the young man is startled and says, "My name is Scott." With a tremble in his voice. Jasmine turns to shut the door and lock it. Jeremy grabs Jasmine by the arm and says, "No, that's enough for one night we should go." Jasmine snatches away from Jeremy, walks up to Scott, and says, "What are you doing here so late?" Scott says, "My dad is the janitor here; I sometimes come to work with him to get a jumpstart on my assignments."

Jasmine runs her fingers through Scott's hair and continues to flirt with him; her eyes begin to glow as she makes eye contact with Scott, hypnotizing him. An unamused Jeremy warps to Jasmine, grabs her by the wrist, and says, "ENOUGH! It's time to go! Michael won't approve of this." Jasmine laughs and turns her attention back to Scott; she leans in to bite his neck.

Jeremy pulls her away and says, "Michael said." Before he could finish, Jasmine pushes Jeremy across the room and says, "Fuck Michael! He can have his pets, then so can I!" Jasmine bites Scott; Scott lets out a scream of agony. The drone picked up his scream, and it pierced John's ear. Scott is now lying on the ground trembling; Jasmine leans over him and says, "You're mine now, little one; if you want to learn how to control this, come to 4561 Madison Drive."

Jasmine and Jeremy turn to smoke and retreat to the mansion. The drone alerts John that it is no longer tracking anyone; John quickly makes a dash toward the school to help the victim he heard screaming. He finds the room where Scott is by locating his drone, but he only finds a pool of blood and no body. John plays back the drone's recording and writes down the address Jasmine told Scott to come to.

At the mansion, Jeremy is fuming with anger, pacing back and forth, and talking to himself: "They're going to find out... no, no, he's going to find out... you crossed the line, you for sure crossed the line this time." Jasmine watches Jeremy go back and forth with himself and says, "Will you calm down already?" Jeremy quickly turns to Jasmine and says, "Don't tell me to calm down!" Jeremy is breathing heavily and clenching his fist. "Are you insane?! What you did back at that school was by far the most ignorant thing you have ever done!"

Jasmine stands up and says, "What I did was for me; it was fun, and I'd do it again." Jeremy replies, "Jasmine, you've been making meaningless kills all night, and to go after that kid after what you did to his father; I mean, what were you thinking?!" Jasmine says, "How about you start hunting by yourself? Stop following me around like a little lost puppy; this is how it will be every night with me from now on." The sound of loud footsteps pauses their conversation; Indigo enters the room and makes her way to the TV.

She turns and looks at Jeremy and Jasmine and says, "Trouble in paradise?" With a big smirk, she turns the TV on and sits on the couch. Jeremy looks at Jasmine and says, "We'll continue this conversation later." From the shadows, Michael appears and says, "No, we'll continue this conversation now." Jeremy and Jasmine look at Michael with fear on their faces. Michael walks over to Jeremy and Jasmine.

He sits down in his throne chair, looking at them with disgust; he takes a deep breath and says, "After you two tried to ambush me earlier, I decided to keep tabs on you myself; I followed the blood trails you left behind, I watched the slaughter, and I noticed the hunter." Jeremy and Jasmine looked at Michael in shock when he said, "Hunter." Michael smirks at the two of them and continues, "Yeah, a hunter was on your trail. Were you that angry that you couldn't detect him?"

Michael stood up and continued, "STUPID AND CARELESS IS WHAT YOU ARE!" Michael lifts his hands and summons what appears to be Scott, the boy Jasmine turned, but he's different somehow, mindless, and rogue. Michael looks at Jasmine with his nose flared up and says, "That janitor you killed, his name was Tom, and this! This is his son! This is why we don't turn children; their adolescent minds and immature nature can't handle the change. They become vampire zombies. LOOK AT HIM!" Scott crawls on the ground, sniffing everything he encounters like a stray dog.

Jasmine, shaken by what she is witnessing, Michael looks at her and says, "Well, what do you have to say for yourself?" Jasmine was completely lost for words. Michael looks at Scott and says, "Your silence tells me everything I need to know." Michael raises his hand and attempts to strike Scott, aiming for his heart. Jasmine quickly warps towards Michael and grabs his hand, stopping his attack. Michael looks at Jasmine and says, "What do you think you're doing?" Jasmine says, "You can't kill him; he's just a kid." Michael snatches away from Jasmine and says, "He doesn't even know what he is! His mind is gone, and it will only worsen from here."

Jasmine looks at Scott and is saddened by what she has done; she looks back at Michael and says, "This is my fault; I take full responsibility; I'll take care of it." Michael says, "I know you will." Jasmine walks towards Scott, "That's not all." Michael says, causing Jasmine to stop in her tracks. While Michael scolded his recruits, Derek put his plan to work. After receiving the Intel John retrieved while following Jeremy and Jasmine, Derek decided to use this information to his advantage.

Derek thinks that if he can expose Michael's true vampire nature to Vanessa, he can convince her to disregard any feelings she may have for him, and he can make the killing of Michael that much sweeter. Derek arrives at Vanessa's home, but before he can knock on the door, it is already being opened; he startled Vanessa. "What are you doing here?" Vanessa said. "Sorry, I didn't mean to scare you, and I know I'm not supposed to be here, but I need to show you something."

Vanessa rolls her eyes and says, "Derek, whatever you think you have to show me, I'm sure it's not really important now please leave before Michael finds out about this." Vanessa brushed past Derek as she walked by, and Derek's tone slightly changed.

He says, "You don't understand Vanessa... you're coming with me."

Derek signals for John and Teddrick. The two of them get out of the car and approach Vanessa. Derek says, "Don't hurt her. Just carefully place her in the car. Vanessa instantly puts up a fight by kneeing John in the groin and smacking Teddrick with her purse; Derek quickly intervenes by grabbing Vanessa. "Trust me, you want to see this." Derek says. John hits Vanessa on the back of the head with the butt of his gun, knocking her out cold, she's placed in the car, and they drive away.

# Chapter Ten

# <u>What should've been the End</u>

The sound of a car engine roaring, guns being loaded, and men talking loudly. Everything Vanessa starts to hear as she regains consciousness. She's looking around the room and realizes she's tied to a chair; she becomes furious and sees Derek talking to one of the men and quickly blurts out, "Are you insane! Where am I? What is all of this?" All the men turn to look at Vanessa. "That's a legit question. Are you insane?!" she continued.

Derek slowly approaches and says, "I think the insane one is you; how can you still love him after knowing what he's become?" Vanessa laughs at Derek and says, "You're obsessed, and it's starting to become really annoying." Derek scoffs and says, "Tell me, Vanessa, how well do you know this new Michael? Have you seen him in his true nature before?" Vanessa replies, "What are you talking about?" Derek calls for John. "This is John. He's our field expert, and he's been tracking things like Michael for some time now, and we would love to show you a presentation." John sets up his projector screen to display what he found while tracking Jasmine and Jeremy.

Derek continues, "Trust me, we're doing this so that you and Kendi can be safe." Vanessa rolls her eyes and sits in silence. John says, "All set, boss." Derek says, "Great, okay, Vanessa, this is the side of Michael you haven't seen, so I need you to pay close attention." What's being shown is the footage the drone collected while John was on patrol.

Vanessa and everyone are watching as the drone follows the man and woman into the school, and suddenly, they disappear. "Where did they go?" Vanessa says. John replies, "They move so fast and quickly use the shadows for cover that my drone couldn't keep up, so now we only have audio. listen." Vanessa says, "Okay, but what does this have to do with Michael?" Derek ignores her and signals John to continue with the audio.

Horrified by what she's hearing, the sound of someone screaming for help, someone being killed. "Turn it off!" Vanessa shouted, but the men continued to let the audio play. Vanessa tried to block out the sound until she heard one of them say Michael's name, quickly catching her attention. As the conversation continued, they heard a woman mention an address, and with that, Derek had the audio stopped. "You see, they have some sort of connection with Michael, and we now have an address of where they might be laying their head."

Vanessa sitting in silence and completely in shock. Derek walks over to her, crouches down, and says, "You, see? He's not the same, even though that wasn't him on the audio doing the killing. He's obviously the one they answer to, so you can't love him." Vanessa still unresponsive and completely ignores Derek as he speaks to her. Derek continues, "I know you're trying to wrap your head around this, Vanessa, and as always, I will be here for you."

Derek touches Vanessa's shoulder and slowly runs his hand down her arm; she turns to Derek, now irritated, and says, "You thought kidnapping me and doing show and tell with your little boy band was going to just make me stop being in his corner?" Vanessa laughs and continues, "Once he finds out you kidnapped me and brought me here against my will, he will kill you." Vanessa gave a menacing smile to Derek, which infuriated him. Derek stands up, angry, and says, "Regardless of how you feel, we're going to kill him tonight! We leave in the next twenty minutes, and when we reach that address, whoever is there will die, starting with him! And you're going to watch." Derek spits on the ground near Vanessa's feet and walks off.

The men are loading their guns and getting their defenses ready as they're getting ready to head into battle, as they call it. "Put her in the back of my truck." Derek says to Teddrick. Unknown to Michael that he is about to have unwanted guests arrive at his home, he also can't sense that Vanessa is in any danger because he is still furious with Jasmine's silly decision she made based off emotions.

Jeremy tells the group, "Michael, we're sorry, Jasmine's emotions were just running high." Jasmine interrupts and says, "Don't speak for me." Jeremy completely ignores her and says, "What about the hunter?" Michael says, "What about him?" Jeremy replies, "Well, what do we do about him." Michael laughs and says, "Well if you two couldn't detect him, what makes you think we can do anything about him? We don't even know who he is." Jeremy says, "Well, there might be another problem." Jeremy took a brief pause.

"Jasmine, well she," Jasmine quickly interrupts and says, "I told Scott where to go; I gave him our address." Indigo stands up now. "So, should we kill her now since she's exposed our location." Jasmine gets defensive and says, "You can try if you want; just know I've been waiting for this opportunity." Michael says, "Stop!" Everyone stops for a moment as Michael begins to speak.

"We must regain our focus; when you're angry, it's hard to mind your surroundings and detect anything, so we'll need to go back to the school and track everywhere you two went, and if you focus hard enough you can trace where the hunter was exactly, we need to pick up on his scent. First, everyone regain their focus, then we can go."

Two trucks approach the mansion, and the men exit both vehicles. "Grab her; make sure she gets a front-row seat." Derek says. John gets Vanessa out of the truck, and they approach the mansion. Michael senses trouble outside of his home, "We have company," he says to everyone. Indigo says, "I sense them too." Jeremy says, "Who are they?" Michael says, "Whoever they are, they aren't welcomed here. Jasmine, take Scott to your room and come back." Jasmine looks at Michael and says, "What are we about to do?" Michael smirks at everyone and says, "We're about to feast."

Then Michael sensed something else, Michael now growing agitated. "They're here." He says; Indigo and Jeremy reply, "Who?" Clinching his fist and shaking, Michael says, "The hunters, and they've brought a hostage." Indigo replies, "Vanessa." Michael says, "It's Derek." Teddrick aims a rocket launcher at the mansion's front door and fires; the vampires quickly warp out of the way and take cover. Michael telepathically tells his team to stick to the shadows. "They can't fight us in the shadows, be swift about every action you take."

Derek tells his men, "Put on your night vision goggles, boys; we know shadows are their favorite element." The men enter the mansion; Derek has Vanessa by the arm as he walks in; he sits her down in the nearest chair. "Here you go, front-row seat." Michael lurking from the shadows, angry at the sight of Derek, even more angry at the fact of him seeing Vanessa in the middle of all of this. "What's that hissing sound?" Todd says. Michael grabs Scott by the neck and throws him at Todd; Scott lands on him and tries to feed. Todd is screaming hysterically, yelling for help.

"I'm coming, Todd!" Teddrick says. Scott bites through Todd's chest, going after his heart; Todd is dying slowly as Scott is feeding on his soon-to-be lifeless corpse. Derek fires a shot, hitting Scott in the head and knocking him off Todd; Derek stands over Scott, stabs him in the heart with a wooden stake, and then chops off his head.

Derek looks up and sees Michael standing halfway out of the shadow. Michael smiles at Derek and disappears in the dark. Derek goes over the radio and tells John to use the UV ray they have right outside of the mansion; before John can turn it on, Jasmine charges at him, striking him down. John quickly gets back up and says, "It's you, where's your friend?" Jasmine says, "You're the hunter?!" John is getting Jasmine in the position of the big glass window before he turns on the UV machine; Jasmine is angry and not paying attention to what's happening.

She's falling for John's trap. Jeremy grabs Teddrick and throws him into the same room where John and Jasmine are. Jeremy enters the room and says, "Well, this should be fun." Jeremy and Jasmine snarled, their mouths watering; they quickly charged at the two men. Teddrick looks at John and yells, "NOW!" John quickly presses the button on his remote, turning on the UV rays outside; as the rays from the machine shine brightly into the mansion's windows, Jeremy, and Jasmine shriek with agony as they are slowly burned to ashes.

Teddrick and John look at each other and are relieved they didn't just become dinner for the immortals. Outside, Michael destroys the machine; he's panting and shaking because he's angry. Indigo enters the room where her colleagues were just killed, a startled John and Teddrick are looking at Indigo with fear in their eyes. She's holding one of their men, Clint, by the neck. "You killed them," she says; she then bites Clint on the neck, splattering his blood onto John and Teddrick.

She drops Clint's lifeless body on the ground, gets in her charging stance, and says, "Now it's your turn to die!" But before she could act, Derek stabbed Indigo in the back, piercing her heart; Michael felt Indigo's pain and is now in full rage. As Derek holds the stake in place where he stabs Indigo, he says, "No, my dear, you're the one that dies."

Derek removes the stake from her chest; Indigo, gasping for air, and drops to the ground. She telepathically tells Michael, "I'm sorry, my love, now show them what fear is, kill them all." Derek strikes Indigo with the axe he used to kill Scott and beheads her. Derek, Teddrick, and John celebrate what they believe is a victory, "Only One left, boys! The big bad Michael," Derek says. Teddrick says, "Well, let's go find him." The men spread out thoroughly searching the mansion, looking for Michael; Michael warps to Vanessa and unties her. "You want a real show? Watch me slaughter them."

Vanessa grabs Michael and says, "This may sound crazy, but save Derek for last." Michael looks at Vanessa and smiles. He quickly warps to where John is; John is in a bedroom, which appears to be Indigo's room. He stumbles across a jewelry box, grabs all the jewelry he sees, and starts stuffing his bag. "So, you like women's jewelry," Michael says; he startles John; John shouts, "He's!" Michael raises his hand at John, and from a distance, he uses his powers to choke him, which prevents John from speaking any further.

Michael walks up to John and bites him, ripping out his throat. Blood sprays everywhere. Michael releases John, and he hits the ground, lying there shaking and dying. "The big bad hunter, now pray to your god and ask him to save you." Michael cuts off John's head and warps to Teddrick. Teddrick is searching for a hidden passageway in the library, knocking books off the shelves; it's unknown to Teddrick that Michael is in the room with him. "So, you like books?" Michael says.

Teddrick grabs his gun, aiming helplessly to figure out who said that. Michael warps in front of Teddrick, startling him. Teddrick falls to the ground. "I asked you a question." Teddrick, shaking, he stands up and says, "So you're Michael." Teddrick aims his gun at Michael's chest and smirks. "You're the reason for all of this." Teddrick says. Michael replies, "I'm the reason none of you are leaving here alive. [Michael continues] You know you smell like her." Teddrick says, "Like who?' Michael says, "Your sister. Lydia" Teddrick fires a shot at Michael, but he misses; after dodging the shot, Michael rushes Teddrick and slashes his throat.

Teddrick drops to his knees and says, "Derek... Derek. Is going to." Michael grabs Teddrick by his hair, and in one pull, he rips Teddrick's head right off his shoulders. Michael then holds Teddrick's head in the air above him and lets the blood spill from his severed head drip into his mouth; he then lowers Teddrick's head and says, "Derek is going to die." Michael exits the library.

Derek calls over the walkie-talkie for his team. "John! Teddrick! What is your location?" No one responds. Derek makes his way to the front door; he reaches into his pocket and pulls out his car keys. Frantically, he drops the keys on the ground. He picks them up, and as he rises, Michael is standing in front of him; Michael punches Derek, and he falls back, knocking him to the ground. Michael says, "Going somewhere?" Derek stands up and says, "So you finally want to face me like a man. Your little freak show didn't stand a chance; we killed them all."

Michael slowly walks towards Derek and says, "Here, catch." Michael throws the severed heads of Derek's team, Teddrick, and John. "Oh, and I found these two along the way." Michael throws the heads of Clint and Todd as well. "All of this bloodshed because you couldn't have Vanessa?" Michael says, Derek responds, "All this bloodshed was necessary because of what you are! You are a monster, Michael!" Vanessa appears behind the wall and says, "What happened to us? We used to be best friends."

Derek replies, "Key words in that sentence used to be. Do you think this was because of her? I did this to protect her; we were well off before you came back, Michael, and it's time you returned to your grave! But take your bride with you this time!" Derek fires a shot at Vanessa, and Michael quickly warps in front of the bullet. Derek's shot Strikes Michael in the shoulder. Michael is furious; his eyes are closed, his fist is clenched, his chest puffing out as he's breathing heavily.

Vanessa calls out his name. "Michael?" she says, but Michael isn't responding; his mind is no longer there. Derek reloads his gun; Michael opens his eyes and looks at Vanessa. She is startled and stands away from him. Michael's eyes go from yellow to solid black with yellow pupils; he looks like he's evolved from a regular vampire. "You're scaring her, Michael," Derek says sarcastically while laughing, holding his fully loaded shotgun. Michael turns to Derek and lets out a roar that shakes the entire building; Derek aims at Michael and fires.

He hits Michael in the chest, but Michael keeps moving forward. Derek fires another shot, hitting Michael in the head, and knocking him off balance, but Michael keeps moving forward. Derek continues to fire shot after shot, bullets continuously hitting Michael, but nothing is happening. Derek is still firing, but his gun is empty.

Michael charges at Derek, hits him, and knocks the shotgun into the air; Derek pulls out a blade and tries to stab Michael. Michael quickly warps behind Derek, punches through his back, and rips a hole into his chest; Michael's arm is now through Derek's body, and in his hand is Derek's heart.

Michael says with a deep Satanic-like voice, "It's time for you to die." Michael crushes Derek's heart and pulls his arm out; Derek falls to the ground. Standing there trying to control his breathing, Michael looks around and becomes overwhelmed by what he sees. Vanessa approaches him and says, "It's over; it's all over Michael." She grabs him by the hand, bringing him back to reality; his eyes return to normal, and he is no longer a "beast." Michael and Vanessa exit the mansion. "Let's go home." Vanessa says to Michael, and he replies, "The sun is rising, and I have to clean all of this up, but I'll come see you tonight."

Hours have passed, and as promised, Michael pays Vanessa a visit; the two of them are sitting in the living room reflecting on the events that took place back at the mansion. "So, now what?" Vanessa says to Michael; he turns to her and says, "That is a good question." The two of them sit there with puzzled faces; Vanessa sits closer to Michael and hugs him. Michael lets out a sigh of relief and says, "I have to figure out another way."

Vanessa looks at Michael and says, "I'm here with you every step of the way." Michael hugs Vanessa, kisses her forehead, and says, "It's late; I should be going now." Vanessa walks Michael to the door before leaving; he says, "Give Kendi a kiss for me." Vanessa smiles and shuts the door. Michael got to the bottom of the steps, and something triggered his senses; there was a danger nearby, but he couldn't pinpoint where it was exactly.

Then suddenly Michael hears a voice: "Beautiful family, Mikey." The voice said. Michael looks up quickly, and in front of him is a figure, but he can't determine who it is. The person steps out of the shadows, and Michael's eyes widen as he is completely shocked by who is standing before him. Michael's shocked look quickly turns into a frown, and he says, "Aries!" Aries smiles back at Michal and says, "You two look great together." Michael warps at Aries and strikes, but he misses, and Aries turns to dust.

Michael turned around, and Aries was behind him. "If you're still trying to kill me, try harder and find better recruits to replace that circus act you were running around with." Aries fades into a black mist and disappears, leaving Michael in the middle of the street, puzzled. Michael warps back to Vanessa's door and knocks loudly and uncontrollably. Vanessa opens the door, and Michael says, "We have a problem."

## The End

Aries and Michael Will Return...